An Etrog from Across the Sea

KERRY OLITZKY *and* DEBORAH BODIN COHEN

illustrated by STACEY DRESSEN MCQUEEN

KAR-BEN
PUBLISHING

For Abraham J. Peck—teacher, colleague, friend
—K.O.

To M & T, with many thanks for your hospitality
—D.B.C.

*With all the love and joy in the world
to Rob, Finn, and Emma*
—S.D.M.

Text copyright © 2024 by Kerry Olitzky and Deborah Bodin Cohen
Illustrations copyright © 2024 by Lerner Publishing Group, Inc.

KAR-BEN PUBLISHING®
An imprint of Lerner Publishing Group, Inc.
241 First Avenue North
Minneapolis, MN 55401 USA
Website address: www.karben.com

Main body text set in Bulmer MT Std Regular.
Typeface provided by Monotype Typography.

Library of Congress Cataloging-in-Publication Data

Names: Olitzky, Kerry M., author. | Cohen, Deborah Bodin, 1968– author. |
    Dressen McQueen, Stacey, illustrator.
Title: An etrog from across the sea / Kerry Olitzky and Deborah Bodin Cohen ;
    illustrated by Stacey Dressen McQueen.
Description: Minneapolis, MN : Kar-Ben Publishing, 2024. | Audience: Ages 4–9. |
    Audience: Grades 2–3. | Summary: Rachel and her family anxiously await Papa's
    return home with the most perfect etrog for Sukkot from across the sea.
Identifiers: LCCN 2023034445 (print) | LCCN 2023034446 (ebook) |
    ISBN 9798765604496 (library binding) | ISBN 9798765632000 (epub)
Subjects: CYAC: Etrog—Fiction. | Sukkot—Fiction. | Family life—Fiction. | Jews—
    United States—Fiction. | New York (State)—History—Colonial period, ca. 1600-
    1775—Fiction. | LCGFT: Picture books.
Classification: LCC PZ7.1.O458 Et 2024 (print) | LCC PZ7.1.O458 (ebook) |
    DDC [Fic]—dc23

LC record available at https://lccn.loc.gov/2023034445
LC ebook record available at https://lccn.loc.gov/2023034446

Manufactured in China
1-1010403-53155-12/19/2023

0924/B2629/A7

July 1729

To my beloved wife and my dear children, Leah and Aaron,

We have been blessed with calm seas across the Atlantic. So
far we have avoided pirates! And I have met many trading
partners here in the Mediterranean.

I write this letter from the island of Corsica, off the coast of France. You will not believe what I found here. Citron trees! The Sukkot fruit that we call the etrog! The farmers here grow the most spectacular etrogs in their orchards.

Still, I yearn for our cozy homestead in the woods. My ship
will reach New York in time for Rosh Hashanah, and I will
bring the finest etrog from Corsica with me. We will celebrate
the New Year and Sukkot together. Please come to the city,
stay with Grandpapa Luis, and meet me at the port.

With much love,
Your devoted Judah (Papa)

Clip-clop, clippety-clop.

The day before Rosh Hashanah, Leah sat in the stagecoach, listening to the rhythm of the horse's steps. She, Aaron, and Mama had woken before dawn to travel from their homestead to the city. Soon they would reach New York. Soon they would see Papa, after six long months!

Grandpapa Luis met them at his fine house. Together,
the family went to the docks to wait for Papa's ship.

But Papa did not come.

"What if something happened to him?" asked Leah.
"A storm? An accident? Pirates?"

"Nothing has happened to him," snapped Aaron.
"His ship's been delayed, that's all."

Leah and Aaron went to the docks every day. But the New Year passed and then Yom Kippur, and Papa did not arrive.

The day after Yom Kippur, Mama said, "I wish we could wait longer. But somebody needs to take care of the mill and the trading post. Papa would want us to go home."

"If Papa arrives, Grandpapa will tell him where we are," said Leah.

"*When* Papa arrives," corrected Aaron.

Before they left the city, Grandpapa Luis said, "Leah, I want you to have something." He held out the delicate silver cup that he'd brought from England years ago. It had been made to store mustard, but Grandpapa Luis used it as an etrog holder on Sukkot.

"Keep this safe for me," Grandpapa Luis told Leah.
"Your papa will return home soon. And he will bring
you an etrog from across the sea to put in this cup."

Clip-clop, clippety-clop.

On the way home, Leah took out the delicate silver cup from her satchel and twirled it in her hand.

Mama gasped, "Why do you have Grandpapa Luis's cup?"

"Did you steal it from his cupboard?" said Aaron.

"Grandpapa gave it to me!"

"Why did he give it to you and not me?" asked Aaron.

Just then, the stagecoach jerked. The cup
flew out of Leah's hands and rolled under
the seat. Aaron grabbed it and held it high,
out of Leah's reach.

"Stop it, children!" said Mama. "Yom Kippur has only just ended. And your papa may be lost at sea. Must you argue?"

Leah sighed. "I'm sorry, Mama. But I promised Grandpapa that I'd keep the cup safe until Papa comes back with an etrog to put in it."

Mama looked out the window, but
Leah saw the tears in her eyes.

The stagecoach stopped, letting them off at their homestead. It was not as fine as Grandpapa Luis's city house, but Leah loved it. She could walk in the forest and swim in the creek. Lenape and Mohican traders visited often with furs to sell, and they'd taught her and Aaron where to fish.

"I wish we'd stayed in the city—at least until Sukkot,"
said Aaron.

"Sukkot is much better here," said Leah. "I didn't
want to eat in a sukkah right next to Grandpapa's
stinky outhouse and stable."

She missed Papa very much.

For the next week, Leah kept herself busy preparing for Sukkot and tried not to think too much about Papa.

She walked in the woods to collect willow branches for a lulav. When she heard birds sing, she remembered Papa's gentle voice. Would he be home to sing the Kiddush over the wine in the sukkah?

"Papa, where are you?" Leah said to the wind.

"How will we be able to build the sukkah without Papa?" Leah asked.

"Don't worry," said Aaron. "I'll build it."

"But you can't do it alone. You'll need help," said Leah.

Together, Mama, Aaron, and
Leah built the sukkah.

Leah put Grandpapa Luis's cup and her
handmade lulav on a small table. The table
looked incomplete without an etrog. And
the family felt incomplete without Papa.

On the first evening
of Sukkot, the family
gathered in the sukkah.
Just as Mama prepared to
light the holiday candles,
Leah heard a noise.

Clip-clop, clippety-clop.

A stagecoach!

Leah ran from the sukkah and jumped into Papa's arms.

"I'm sorry to be so late," said Papa. "We had to dock in Nova Scotia for repairs. But I am here for Sukkot—and I brought an etrog from Corsica, just as I promised!"

The etrog was bright yellow like the sun. Leah
smelled its sweet scent and felt its finely textured skin.

"It's the most perfect etrog I've ever seen," she
whispered, placing it in Grandpapa Luis's cup.

"And tonight begins the most perfect Sukkot," said Papa.

And, for once, Leah and Aaron agreed.

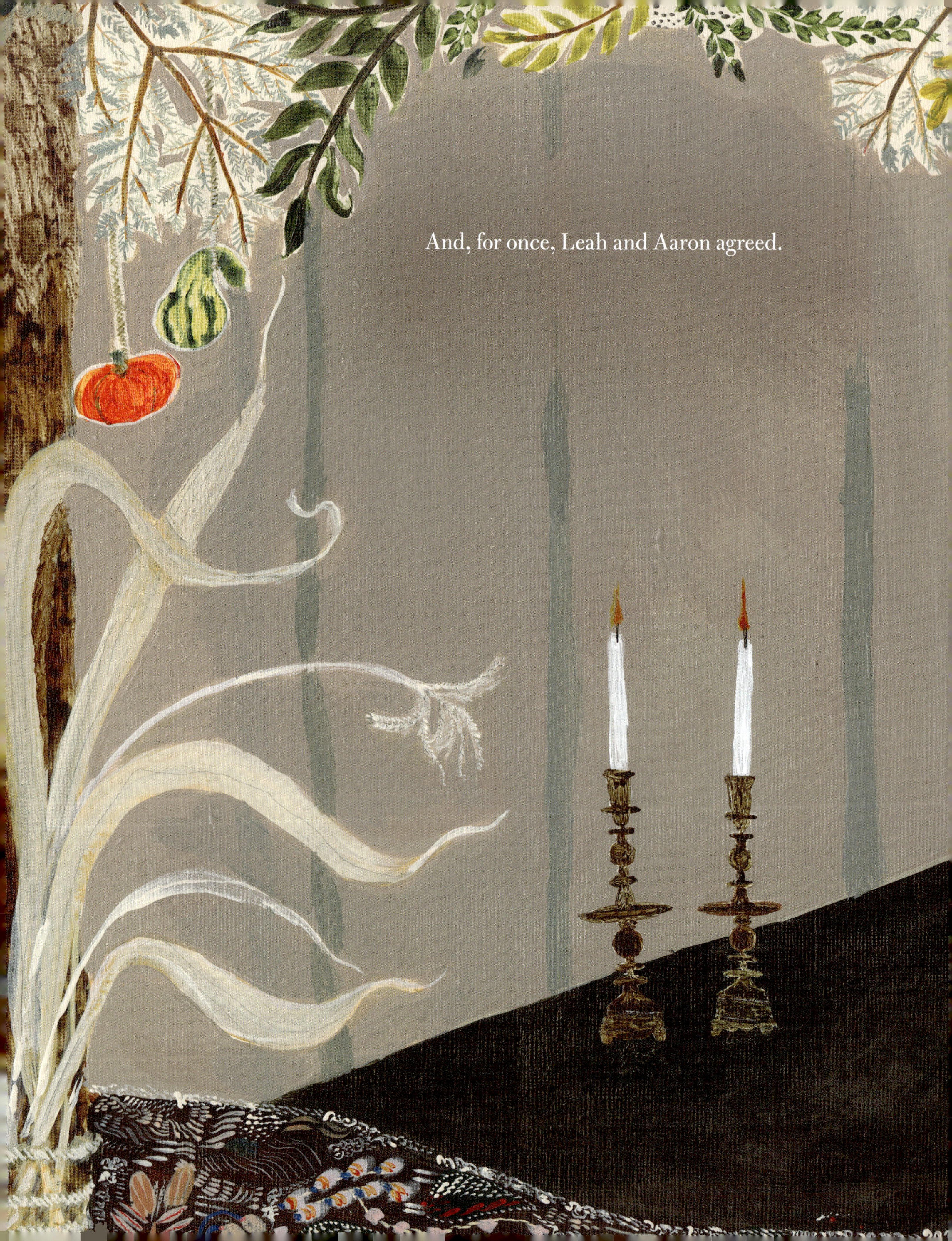